Lerato Cooks Up a Plan

A Green Engineering Story

Written by the Engineering is Elementary Team

Illustrated by Ross Sullivan-Wiley

Chapter One | Fetching Firewood

I squinted my eyes and looked into the distance. Though the sun was setting, waves of heat sizzled from the white sand under my feet. I shifted my arm to lift Baruti higher on my hip, being careful not to drop the firewood I'd bundled and balanced on my head. "Where do you think they've gone, little brother?" I asked, scanning the plain for Sibanda and Kagiso, my brother and sister.

Baruti tilted his head, gazing seriously at me with wide brown eyes, as if to say, "I don't know." I laughed. Baruti was too young to talk with words, but he always seemed to communicate with his eyes. And I talked back to him, especially when it was just the two of us. "Should we go look for them by the river?" I asked as we walked. "I told them we had to get back as soon as we could. I bet the party's already started at home." I sighed. "I guess this is what I get for never listening to Dekeledi when I was younger. Now Kagiso and Sibanda do the same thing to me."

I'd only taken a few steps when I stopped short. Baruti grunted as he thumped against my side. "Sorry," I said. "But look at those palm fronds." I pointed toward a squat bunch of fronds fanning out from a bush by the river. "They'd be perfect for my next basket, especially with a red dye. I wonder if I should cut some off . . ." I looked up just as two small figures appeared in the distance. "It seems like there's never time for basket weaving anymore. Maybe we can come back for these later."

I hurried to meet Sibanda and Kagiso. Sibanda's arms

were full of branches—he hadn't learned to balance them on his head yet. They rose high out of his arms and blocked his face. I could see his legs below, making him look like a tiny tree scurrying toward me. When I caught Kagiso's eye, she picked up her pace.

"Let me guess," I called as they got closer. "Hide and seek? Chasing flamingoes on the salt pans?"

"We played in the river!" Sibanda said, craning his neck to look from behind the branches with a huge grin.

"Sibanda!" Kagiso cried, her eyebrows forming an angry V. She poked Sibanda's side with her elbow, but he kept looking at me with his goofy smile.

I wanted to giggle, but I knew I should be stern. I kept my mouth in a frown and tried to act like . . . well, like

Dekeledi, our older sister, acted when she used to take care of us.

"You can't keep running off every time we come to collect firewood," I said. "It can be dangerous near the river. You wouldn't do that if Dekeledi were here." Now that Dekeledi had finished high school, she had a job at the medical clinic, and it was my turn to watch our younger brothers and sister. I'd only been "in charge" for a few months, and sometimes I thought I wasn't very good at it. Kagiso was only two years younger than I was. And I had to admit that a few times when Dekeledi had brought us to gather firewood, I had snuck off with Kagiso and Sibanda to walk in the cool water. But I couldn't do things like that anymore.

"Lerato, we barely stuck our toes in the river—and we were gathering branches the whole time," Kagiso said. "You know we hate gathering firewood. Stopping at the river makes it a little bit more fun. Please don't tell Grandma and get us in trouble."

"Okay, okay," I said. "I won't tell her." At that, Sibanda smiled again. "But that better be the last time you sneak off when we're doing chores. Let's get back and go to the party."

Chapter Two | Tsoane's Party

As we neared Nata, our village, I heard music and laughter. I'd been right—the party had already begun. We were all celebrating Tsoane's homecoming. She'd been away at university for the past few months, and I'd missed her. Tsoane was good friends with Dekeledi, but she had spent a lot of time with me, too. Tsoane and I had a special connection because we both wove baskets. Sometimes when we wove together she would teach me new patterns.

"Do you think Tsoane is glad to be home?" Kagiso asked me.

"I'm sure she is," I said. Now that we were close enough to hear the excitement, we walked a bit faster. "Wouldn't you be happy to have a party when you came home from university?"

Kagiso reshuffled the branches in her arms, tilted her head, and looked into the distance. "Well . . . I like parties," she said, "but I don't know if I'd want to go to university. I think I'd be sad to leave Nata. Do you think you'll go to university?" Kagiso asked me.

"I've never thought about it," I said quickly. "Come on. We're almost home."

Sibanda ran in front of me, and Kagiso followed. I felt Baruti's soft eyes staring intently at me. "I know, I know," I said, looking down at him. "I do want to go to university. But if I tell Kagiso, she'll be sure to tell Dekeledi and Grandma."

Sometimes Dekeledi read me parts of the letters Tsoane sent home to her. Tsoane wrote about her classes and about living in Gaborone—the capital of Botswana. Tsoane was

studying green engineering. I knew when she wrote about green engineering that she didn't mean the color. It had something to do with the *tikologo*—environment—and with technologies. In one of her letters she explained that technologies are any things, systems, or processes that people design to help solve problems. I wanted to ask Tsoane more about

green engineering and about university when I saw her.

"Dekeledi is very busy at the clinic," I said aloud, mostly to myself, "and in a few years when I'll be ready to leave for school, she'll have her own family. Grandma will need me here, not away at university. I could probably earn money for the family by selling some of my baskets—if I ever get time to work on them." I sighed.

"Dah," Baruti said, putting his little hand on my cheek.

"That's very nice of you," I said back to him. "Don't worry. I know that going to university is just a dream."

I set down my pile of firewood on top of the stack Kagiso and Sibanda had made, and grabbed the basket I'd filled earlier with berries to bring to the party. The basket with its flower pattern was one of my favorites. It had taken me days to get it just right. "Let's go find Tsoane," I said to Baruti.

I spotted Dekeledi's bright headscarf first, then Tsoane's wide smile. I caught Dekeledi's eye and she waved me over. "Welcome back, Tsoane," I said. "How are you?"

"Glad to be home," Tsoane said, giving me a hug. "Look at Baruti! So much bigger than the last time I saw him. You look taller, too, Lerato. Oh, did you make that basket? I can't wait to tell you all about school!"

I giggled. Tsoane was always like that—talking and thinking two steps ahead of everyone else.

"Dekeledi read me parts of your letters about university," I told Tsoane. "Everything there sounds so exciting. Do you like living there?"

"I do," Tsoane said. "It's very different from Nata."

"Is it true that everyone in the city has electricity?" Dekeledi asked.

"A lot of the homes and buildings do," Tsoane said. "And there are so many computers in the university library."

"Are the computers the technologies you design?" I asked. "In one of your letters you said that engineers design technologies."

"Computers, and lots of other technologies, could be

designed using green engineering," Tsoane said. "Almost all technologies—from a book to a basket to the *rondavels* we live in—impact the environment in some way. Green engineering means that the technology, whatever it might be, was designed to impact the environment as little as possible."

"How do you know how something impacts the environment?" I asked.

"Sometimes it can be hard to figure out," Tsoane said. "One tool we use is called a life cycle assessment. By looking at the life of a technology, we can identify all the resources

needed to make it, how much energy is used, and whether pollution or waste are created. Those things give us clues about whether something is a green technology. "

"The life of a technology?" Dekeledi asked. "I don't know what they're teaching you at university, but last I knew, books and baskets and *rondavels* were not alive."

Tsoane laughed. "I know they're not alive," she said. "I suppose it is a funny way to talk about objects. Think of it like this: we make, use, and dispose of technologies. Those stages are sort of the way a technology grows up. Lots of resources—people, machines, and energy—can go into making even simple technologies. And depending on the technology, it might impact the *tikologo* with pollution or waste or—"

"Tsoane, there you are," Tsoane's mother said as she crossed the yard. She placed a hand on Tsoane's shoulder. "Come say hello to Mr. and Mrs. Wanjala."

"I'll be right over," Tsoane said. She shrugged her shoulders as she turned back to us. "I think I've said hello to every person in this village!" she said. Dekeledi laughed.

"Why don't you come have tea with us tomorrow?" Dekeledi asked.

"That sounds great!" Tsoane said. "I'll see you then."

Chapter Three | Thinking About Resources

The next morning I woke up extra early—even before the sun had appeared on the horizon. As soon as my eyes opened I started thinking about what Tsoane had said—that green technologies were designed to minimize their impact on the environment. I laid on my back for a few moments, staring up at the thatched roof of the *rondavel*. Tsoane had said looking at the life cycle of something can give clues about how green it is. But the more I thought about resources and pollution and waste, the more my head felt cloudy and confused. A gurgle from Baruti let me know he was awake, too.

I picked up Baruti and went outside to start the day. "Maybe we can figure this out together," I whispered to

Baruti. "Do you want to help me?" Baruti's barely awake, sleepy eyes didn't seem very excited.

I took a handful of branches and set them on the ashes of yesterday's fire. "Let's try thinking about the fire as an example," I said to Baruti. "We need the branches to create the fire. They must be a resource." Baruti let out a yawn. "I guess we're resources, too," I said to him, "since Kagiso and Sibanda and I help to gather the wood." I picked up a match and struck it against one of the rocks at the edge of the fire pit. "Another resource," I said, holding it up for Baruti to

see. As the fire glowed and the light of the sun started to creep through the village, Baruti's eyes opened wider.

"Now what are the impacts on the environment?" I took a moment to think. "The trees are impacted." I looked off in the distance as I continued to think out loud. "We use a lot of branches each day. It takes a long time for new branches to grow on trees." I watched the smoke billow and dance as it floated upwards. "The fire creates smoke, so that must be another impact on the environment."

I knew I would still have a few minutes to myself before

everyone else woke up. I reached for the basket I'd started to weave a few days before.

"I wonder if any of this is right," I said. "What would a real engineer say about the life cycle of a fire? Is it a green technology? I'll have to ask Tsoane about that later."

Chapter Four | Tea Time

I had only been home from school a few moments when I heard Kagiso and Sibanda calling to me. "Tsoane is coming!"

I pulled three wooden stools to the fire, where I'd set the teapot to warm. Dekeledi, Tsoane, and I sat down.

"Sibanda, don't touch!" Dekeledi and I said at the same time. Sibanda pulled his hand away from the pot.

Dekeledi laughed. "I guess you really are in charge now," she said to me.

I couldn't help smiling proudly as I poured the tea. "I'm trying," I said. "But I still haven't been able to keep Sibanda and Kagiso away from the river when we're collecting branches."

"I never liked going to collect firewood," Tsoane said. "Now I kind of miss gathering branches and making a fire."

"I would never miss that," Sibanda said solemnly. "I wish I lived in the city."

"There are lots of good things about living in Gaborone," Tsoane said, "but I wish some of Nata's traditions could be found in the city."

"Like what?" Dekeledi asked.

"Well, our *rondavels*, for instance," she said, pointing at our home. "They stay much cooler than many of the homes in the city."

"But you said the homes in the city all have electricity and water," Dekeledi countered.

"That's true," Tsoane said, "but my dorm room at

university gets much hotter than the inside of a *rondavel*. When I get home from classes and open my door, I feel a blast of hot air."

"Yuck," Sibanda said.

"Why are the dorms so hot?" I asked.

"The roof of my dorm is made of metal," Tsoane said. "Metal is a thermal conductor. It transfers the heat energy from outside into the building quickly. The dorm roofs aren't well matched to a place as sunny and hot as Botswana."

"*Rondavel* roofs are made of grass," Kagiso said. "Is that what keeps them cool?"

"That's right. Air gets trapped in the spaces between the grass, and that helps insulate the *rondavels* and keep them cool," Tsoane said. "The thick mud walls help, too. Both the

grass and the mud are good thermal insulators—they transfer heat energy slowly. That means the heat from outside the *rondavel* can't quickly move through the roof and the walls to the inside."

"No wonder we've made the *rondavels* the same way for so many years," I said. "Grandma said the way she taught me to make *rondavels* is the same way her grandmother taught her."

"Yes," Tsoane said. "We can keep building them the same way because the *rondavels* are sustainable—they're

a good match for our environment and for the people of Botswana. The mud and grass are local resources, and they're natural materials, so they don't have much negative impact on the *tikologo*. The materials we use to build the *rondavels* don't create pollution or waste. The heat energy we use from the sun to dry the mud, and the energy from people working to build the *rondavel*, won't hurt the environment, either."

"Tsoane," I interrupted. "What about our cooking fire? I was thinking about it this morning. The branches we use are natural resources, but they're harder and harder to find."

"It's true!" Kagiso said. "We used to be able to get them right outside of the village. Now those trees are all bare. We have to walk all the way to the river to gather branches now. "

"Does that mean using the branches to make our fire isn't a green choice?" I asked.

"That's a great observation," Tsoane said. "Even though the branches are a local resource, we have used so many of them that now they are hard to find. Nata isn't the only village with this problem. In fact, we talked about this at university. I might have something that could help. Wait here—I will show it to you. I'll be right back."

Chapter Five | Cooking with the Sun?

Tsoane came back with a big box, which she set on the ground. I looked at the box closely, but I still wasn't sure what it was.

"It's a solar oven!" Tsoane said, as if reading my thoughts. "The oven uses energy from the sun to cook food."

"This box can cook food?" I asked. I was holding Baruti, and he reached out toward the box. "Don't touch," I said out of habit. "Is it hot?" I asked, realizing it might not be the same as our cooking fire.

"It's not hot right now, but if you use it correctly, the inside can get hot," Tsoane said. "There are a few different parts that help make it work."

Kagiso ran up beside me. "It's a box!" she said. Sibanda joined us on the other side.

"Right," Tsoane said. "The box is one part. Then there's the reflector." She opened up the lid of the oven. "See?"

"Oooh," I said, reaching out to touch the smooth, shiny surface inside.

"And there's a pot!" Sibanda said, grabbing the cooking pot from the box and setting it on his head. He walked in a circle around us, balancing the pot.

"You're silly," I said. "Give that back to Tsoane." I sat down and pulled Sibanda into my lap next to Baruti.

"The metal on the inside of the lid reflects sunlight into the oven, and the clear plastic covering the top traps the heat inside," Tsoane said. "We just have to make sure the lid is at the best angle to catch the sun's rays." As she moved the lid, sunshine created a pool of light in the bottom of the pot.

"So when you put food in the pot, the light and heat energy from the sun cook the food?" I asked.

"Right," Tsoane said. "And the cooking pot is black metal that absorbs heat really well. It's a thermal conductor, just like the roof of my dorm. The pot transfers heat to the food and warms it up."

"That's pretty smart," I said. "How did you know how to make it?"

"I used the engineering design process to help me," Tsoane said. "It's a series of steps that you can use to solve

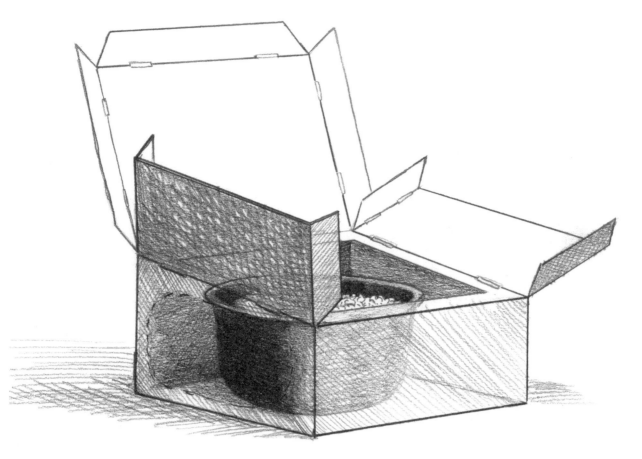

problems. I asked questions, imagined solutions, made a plan, and then created the oven. I tested my first design, but it didn't work very well, so I had to improve it. All those steps are part of the engineering design process."

"And the solar oven works now?" Sibanda asked.

"Why don't you test it yourself?" Tsoane asked. "Should I leave it for you to try?"

"Yes!" Kagiso said. She brought over a bowl of water. "I want to heat this water for tea. How long will it take?"

"When we tested our solar ovens in class, it took about

three hours to cook maize porridge," Tsoane said.

"Three hours!" Kagiso cried. "I can't wait that long!"

"Shush," I said, laughing. "You act like we didn't just have tea."

"But why wouldn't you just heat it over the fire? It's so much easier," Kagiso persisted.

"You just light the fire and cook things," Sibanda agreed.

"What?" I cried. "If only it were that easy. The fire has a life cycle. What do we have to do every evening to make sure we can cook the next day?"

Sibanda crinkled his nose. "Collect firewood!"

"Right," I said. "We collect the firewood, so we are a resource. The branches and the energy from the fire are also resources we need to cook the food."

"That's right," said Tsoane. "And then there are the environmental impacts."

"Like smoke?" I asked.

"Right," Tsoane said. "Smoke is one of the fire's impacts on the environment."

So I had been right! I couldn't help smiling.

"And then once all the firewood has burned, we have to start all over again," Sibanda said, frowning.

"One of the things that makes this solar oven a green

technology is that it uses the energy of the sun to help you cook the food," Tsoane said. "The solar oven uses different resources than the fire. As long as the sun's energy is available as a resource, the solar oven will work."

"And it won't create smoke, either, so there would be fewer impacts on the environment," I said.

"Exactly," Tsoane said. "And you won't have to spend as much time or energy gathering firewood."

"I can't wait to try it!" I declared.

Chapter Six | Testing the Oven

Early the next morning, I poured water into the cooking pot and set it inside the solar oven. Before leaving for school, I showed Sibanda and Kagiso how to angle the oven toward the sun so that it would catch the most sunlight. I couldn't wait to see how it would work.

That afternoon, as I walked toward the *rondavel* for tea, I smiled at the scene. Sibanda and Kagiso were flitting around like birds. Even Baruti sat near the solar oven, curious about what had happened. "Come on!" Kagiso said. I followed her and knelt next to the solar oven. Kagiso gave me a cup, and I used a ladle to pour some of the water from the oven into it. "Did it work, Lerato?" Kagiso asked.

"Here," I said, guiding her hand to the outside of the

cup. "Can you feel how warm it is?" I asked.

"I want to feel!" Sibanda said, touching his hand to the other side of the cup. "Oooh, it is warm."

I nodded. "I don't know if it's quite hot enough to steep the tea, though," I said. "Did you move the oven so it was always angled at the sun?"

"Well . . . it might not have been angled correctly the whole day," Kagiso admitted. I stood, putting my hand on my hip and raising an eyebrow. "We did move it some, Lerato," Kagiso said quickly. "I know we had it facing the sun during the middle of the day when the light is strongest."

"Did we ruin it?" Sibanda asked.

"No, it's not ruined," I said. "But I think we can improve the design." I sat back on my heels and thought for a few moments.

"What are you thinking, Lerato?" Sibanda asked.

"I was remembering what Tsoane had said about her dorm room. She said when she gets home at night and opens the door she feels the hot air rush out."

"I remember that, too!" Kagiso said.

"Right," I said. "She said some materials are thermal insulators and transfer heat energy slowly. I wonder if there's a way to trap more of the heat energy from the sun inside the box. We could use a thermal insulator. I bet we can use the engineering design process to figure it out."

Chapter Seven | A Green Solution

"Here, Lerato!" Sibanda said, handing me an armful of plastic bags. "I bet this would be a good therm-sulator!"

"Thermal insulator," I corrected. I recognized the bags from supplies Dekeledi had bought for the medical clinic. "The bags might be a good insulator. We'll have to ask some good questions about which materials are the best thermal insulators. Tsoane said engineers designing green technologies ask questions, remember? Like questions about where the resources come from?"

"Oh yeah," Kagiso said. "Tsoane said things that we can find easily in Nata might be more green."

"I just thought of something!" I said. "How about using the palm fronds left over from my basket weaving? I bet they would act like the grass roofs on our *rondavels* and trap air in the spaces between them.”

“Mud keeps the rondavels cool, too,” Sibanda said. “We could use mud.”

“All of those sound like good ideas,” I said. “We can test each material separately—one each day. By the end of the week, I bet we’ll be able to tell which worked best!”

Every evening when I got home, Kagiso and Sibanda were waiting to show me how the testing for that day’s material had gone. Some of the materials worked much better than others. We started to imagine combinations of materials and tested to see if those made a difference in how hot the solar oven got. We crumpled some of the materials and re-tested them. Once we figured out which materials worked best, we drew a plan and created our design. Finally, we tried to improve the insulation by adding more material to the box. By the end of the week, we had found a material that we thought would insulate the solar oven well enough so that we could cook a whole pot of maize porridge.

“I want to put the maize in!” Sibanda said.

“Here, I’ll help you pour it,” I said, carefully lifting the bucket so it didn’t spill everywhere.

“Can I add the water?” asked Kagiso.

“Sure,” I said. “Just add it slowly.”

"Lerato, you should go to university and study green engineering, just like Tsoane," Kagiso said.

"You think so?" I asked.

"Yeah," she said. "You are so good at engineering and solving problems. You could go to school and then come back to Nata to teach everyone what you learned."

Sibanda rested his chin on Kagiso's shoulder as she poured the water. "We told Grandma and Dekeledi and all

the other kids in the village about the solar oven," he said.

"And I told them how I want to be just like you when I grow up!" Kagiso said. She set the bucket down and looked up at me.

"Really?" I asked. I could feel myself blushing. "Thanks, Kagiso."

"This must be the solar oven," I heard from behind us. I turned to see Dekeledi and Tsoane.

"Come see," Sibanda said, jumping up to take their hands. Sibanda and Kagiso told them all about the testing we'd done and the insulator we chose. Sibanda was even able to say "thermal insulator" all by himself.

"You did exactly what real engineers do," Tsoane said. "You used the engineering design process to help design a thermal insulator for the solar oven."

"Lerato, when you go to university you should study green engineering just like Tsoane does," Dekeledi said.

"Maybe . . . if I go to university," I said, looking down and fussing with the button on Baruti's shirt.

"What do you mean, if you go?" Dekeledi asked. "Grandma has always wanted you to go to university."

"I need to be here to help take care of everyone," I protested.

"But don't you see?" Dekeledi said. "If you go to school and learn about things like green engineering, you can

come back and do an even better job of helping to take care of us. You could help take care of everyone in Nata."

A few days later I went to say goodbye to Tsoane. She had her bag packed and was ready to return to university.

"I couldn't let you leave without giving you this," I said, handing Tsoane a basket I'd made.

"It's beautiful!" Tsoane said. "I'll keep it in my room."

"Now that we are using the oven and we don't have to collect firewood every day, I've had a lot more time to weave," I said. "Grandma thinks I might even be able to sell some of my baskets to save money for university."

"That's great, Lerato," Tsoane said.

"I made this one especially for you," I said. "The pattern on the basket is a flamingo. It kind of reminds me of you."

"It does?" Tsoane asked, turning her head to look at it better.

"Not the way it looks," I said, giggling. "It's what the flamingoes around Nata do. They leave the nest, but they always come back home. That's like what you're doing—going to university and then coming back home to help people in Nata. I want to do that someday, too."

Design a Solar Oven

Can you design insulation for a solar oven so you can melt s'mores? Your goal will be to build a solar oven, and test different insulators to find out which works best.

Materials

- ☐ Shoebox
- ☐ Aluminum foil
- ☐ Paper bowl
- ☐ Duct tape
- ☐ Thermometer
- ☐ Newspaper
- ☐ Leaves
- ☐ Clear plastic bag
- ☐ Other materials to use as insulators
- ☐ Graham crackers
- ☐ Marshmallows
- ☐ Chocolate

Build Your Solar Oven

Prepare your solar oven. Cut a flap out of the lid of a shoebox. Line the flap with aluminum foil. This will help you reflect the light of the sun into your cooking pot. Cover the hole you cut in the shoebox lid with the clear plastic bag. Seal the edges with duct tape. Cover any other holes in the shoebox with duct tape. Why do you think it is important to cover the holes in the shoebox? Place the bowl—your cooking pot—in the middle of the box.

Ask and Imagine Materials

What materials do you think might be good thermal insulators? Try testing newspaper, leaves, aluminum foil, and other materials you find around the house. Are some materials greener choices than others? Test each material one at a time. Fill the area around your cooking pot with one of the materials. You might want to try crumpling the material or shredding it. Place the thermometer in the cooking pot so that you can see it through the window. Record the starting temperature inside the solar oven. Put your solar oven in the sun for half an hour. Record the temperature after half an hour. How much warmer is the solar oven than when you first took the temperature?

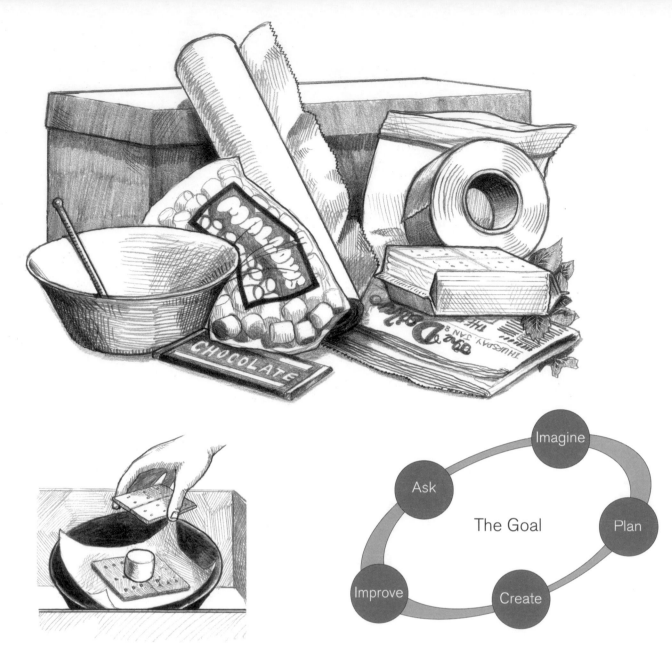

Plan and Create Your Design

Choose the best thermal insulator of all the materials you tested, or use a combination of materials. Draw a plan for your solar oven design to show exactly how much material you plan to use, where it will go, and whether it will be crumpled, shredded, or layered. Put some of the clear plastic in the bottom of the cooking pot so your s'mores don't stick to the pot. Cook a marshmallow on one of the graham crackers. Once your marshmallow melts, add a piece of chocolate and the other cracker.

Improve Your Solar Oven

Can you improve your solar oven so that it gets even warmer? Can you change the shape of the materials so they work better, or change the way you place the materials in your design? Does adding more material or taking some away make a difference? Go to the library or use the Internet to learn more about different types of solar oven designs.

Glossary

Energy: The ability to create change.

Engineer: A person who uses his or her creativity and understanding of mathematics and science to design things that solve problems.

Engineering design process: The steps that engineers use to design something to solve a problem.

Green engineering: The field of engineering concerned with designing technologies that have minimal impact on the environment.

Heat transfer: The movement of heat energy from a hotter substance to a cooler substance.

Life cycle assessment: The process of identifying all the resources needed to create a technology and the effects on the environment resulting from the technology through its lifetime.

Maize porridge: A soft food made by boiling cornmeal until it is thick.

Nata: A village of about 5,000 people located close to the northeastern border of Botswana. Pronounced *NAH-tah*.

Rondavel: A type of home found in some countries in southern Africa. The walls are usually made from rocks and a sand/soil mortar, and the roof is made from tree branches and grass thatch. Pronounced *rahn-DAH-vul.*

Technology: Any thing, system, or process that people create and use to solve a problem.

Thermal insulator: A material that transfers heat energy slowly.

Thermal conductor: A material that transfers heat energy quickly.

Tikologo: Setswana (the language commonly spoken in Nata) word for environment. Pronounced *tee-KOH-low-goh.*

Lerato's Family & Friends

Lerato (Leh-RAH-toe)

Lerato's Sisters

Kagiso, Lerato's younger sister
(Kah-GEE-soh)

Dekeledi, Lerato's older sister
(deh-KEH-led-ee)

Lerato's Brothers

Sibanda, Lerato's younger brother
(SEE-bahn-dah)

Baruti, Lerato's baby brother
(BAH-roo-tee)

Lerato's Friend

Tsoane, Lerato's friend
(so-AH-nay)